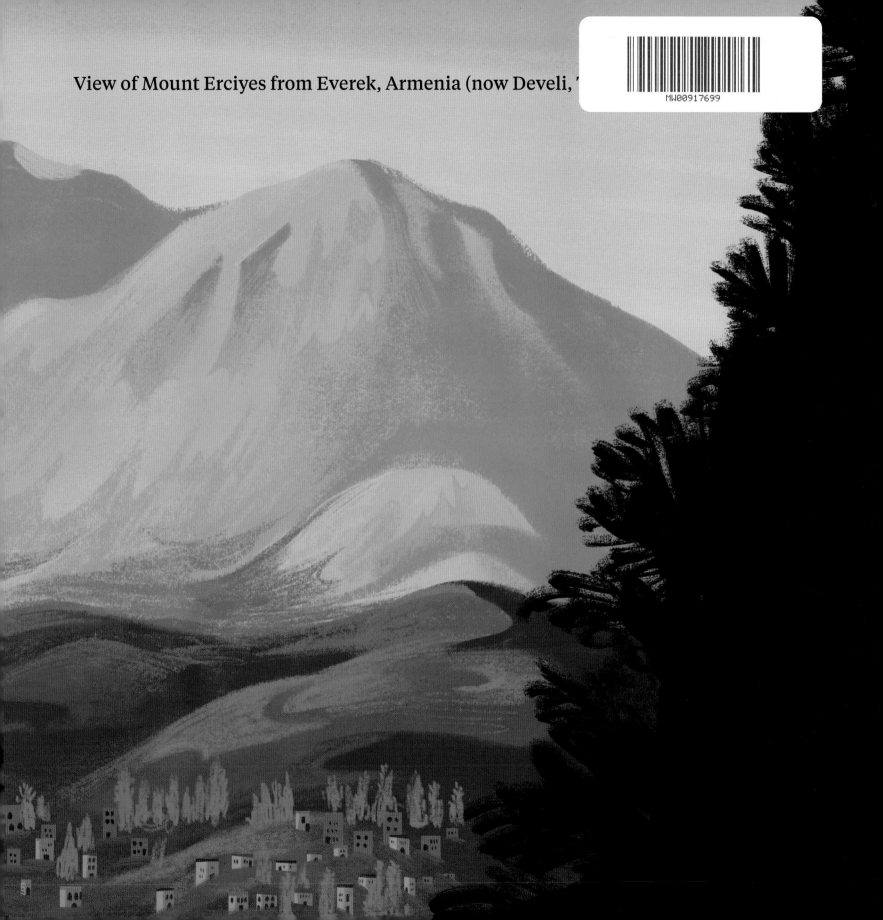

View of Mount Erciyes from Everek, Armenia (now Develi,

Eternal thanks—
first and foremost, to Haig. This book is for you.
To my beautiful boys, for your endless love and support.
To my writing family, for your patience, guidance, and friendship.
To my Armenian family and friends, for sharing your stories with me.
To Elizabeth and Hannah, for believing in this story and helping me share it.
—L. B.

For my loving family.
—S. A.

Library of Congress Cataloging-in-Publication Data

Names: Boukarim, Leila, author. | Avedikian, Sona, illustrator.
Title: Lost words : an Armenian story of survival and hope / written by Leila Boukarim ;
illustrated by Sona Avedikian.
Other titles: An Armenian story of survival and hope
Description: San Francisco : Chronicle Books, 2024. |
Includes bibliographical references. | Audience: Ages 5-8.
Identifiers: LCCN 2023001399 | ISBN 9781797213651 (hardcover)
Subjects: LCSH: Armenians--Turkey--History--20th century--Juvenile fiction. |
Armenians--Lebanon--Juvenile fiction. | Refugees--Armenia--Juvenile
fiction. | Orphans--Juvenile fiction. | Armenian Genocide,
1915-1923--Juvenile fiction. | CYAC: Armenians--Turkey--History--20th
century--Fiction. | Armenians--Lebanon--Fiction. | Refugees--Fiction. |
Orphans--Fiction. | Armenian Genocide, 1915-1923--Fiction. | LCGFT:
Historical fiction. | Picture books.
Classification: LCC PZ7.1.B6777 Lo 2024 | DDC [Fic]--dc23
LC record available at https://lccn.loc.gov/2023001399

Manufactured in China.

Design by Mariam Quraishi and Sandy Frank.
Typeset in Tiempos Text.
The illustrations in this book were rendered digitally.

10 9 8 7 6 5 4 3 2 1

Chronicle Books LLC
680 Second Street
San Francisco, California 94107
www.chroniclekids.com

An Armenian Story of Survival and Hope

Lost Words

Written by Leila Boukarim

Illustrated by Sona Avedikian

chronicle books · san francisco

The smell of parsley and pepper filled the air as Mama and I made mante, pinching dough into tiny boats.

I didn't see it coming . . .

A knock at the door. A conversation in whispers.
Mama's voice was low and urgent.

"You must leave with the others," she pleaded
with me and my sisters.
"What about you, Mama? What about Baba?"
"I will wait for him," she said. "We will follow you."

She dressed us in ragged shirts with gold buttons sewn on the inside.
"In case you need them," Mama whispered in my ear. "Hokis."
She filled our pockets with nuts and dried figs. It was all we took with us.

There was so much I wanted to say, but I had lost my words.

Our long journey began. I looked back,
hoping Mama was right behind us.

"We have to keep going," my sisters insisted.

In the heat and through the dust, we walked.
The sun burned my skin and dried my throat.
The desert stretched out before us, a sea of
sand, with no beginning and no end.

We walked for days.

For weeks.

For months.

I held on to Mama's words like a prayer
and put one foot in front of the other.

Until . . .

Finally, we reached a land with blankets and water and food.

A land far from Mama.

We shared a home with many children.
Some told me their stories and waited for me
to tell mine.

There was so much I wanted to say,
but I had lost my words.

I waited for Mama to join us.

I waited for days.
For weeks.
For months.

"I want to go back" was all I could say.
"There is nothing for us to go back to,"
my sisters would reply.

For a long time, I refused to believe them.
I lay awake, night after night, waiting for
Mama.

When I closed my eyes, I saw her face,
smelled her clothes, heard her voice.
"Hokis."
I was safe here, but this life felt like
a shirt that no longer fit.

As I got bigger,
my pain got smaller.

When I closed my eyes,
Mama was still there,
but she was so far away
I could hardly see her.
Her voice a distant echo.
Her smell gone.

I kept one gold button close,
warm against my skin,
to keep her from disappearing.

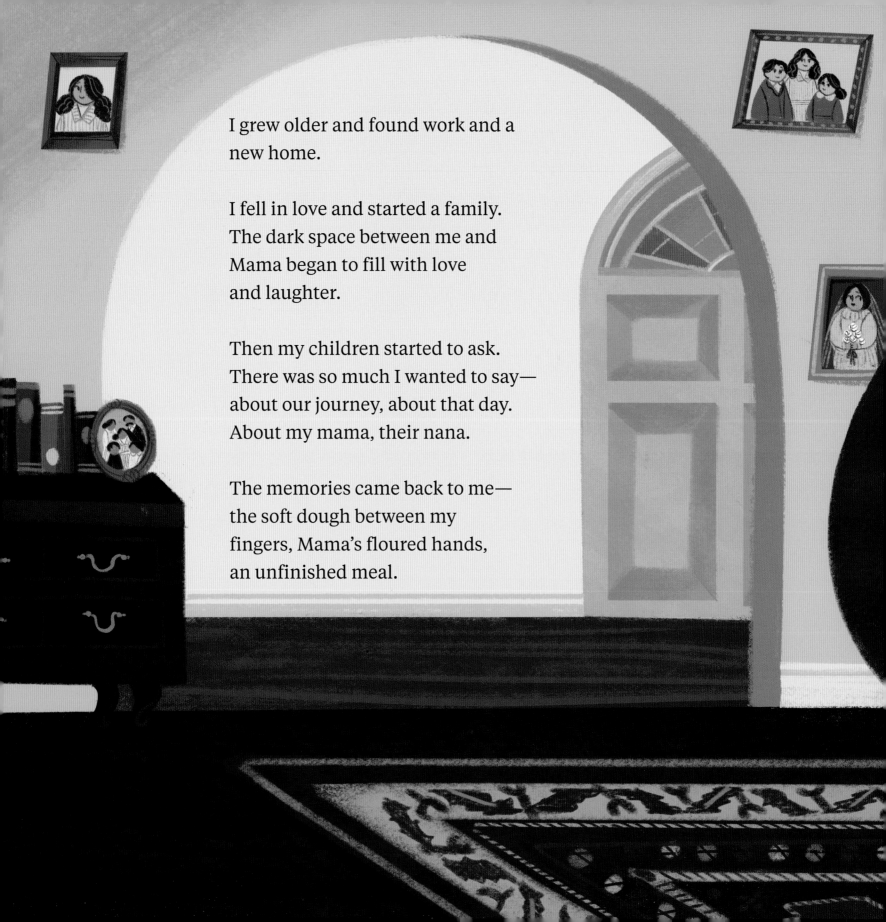

I grew older and found work and a
new home.

I fell in love and started a family.
The dark space between me and
Mama began to fill with love
and laughter.

Then my children started to ask.
There was so much I wanted to say—
about our journey, about that day.
About my mama, their nana.

The memories came back to me—
the soft dough between my
fingers, Mama's floured hands,
an unfinished meal.

But I stayed quiet.
For weeks.
For months.
For years.

I had lost my words.

As the smell of parsley and pepper filled the air and our fingers pinched dough into tiny boats, the question came again.

"Where are we from, Dada?"

I didn't see it coming.
I found my words, dusty from years of
sitting in the dark, unspoken.

I told him, my hokis, about my brave mama and
our march through the desert. About all that
was lost and all that we treasure. About our food,
our culture, our music, our stories.

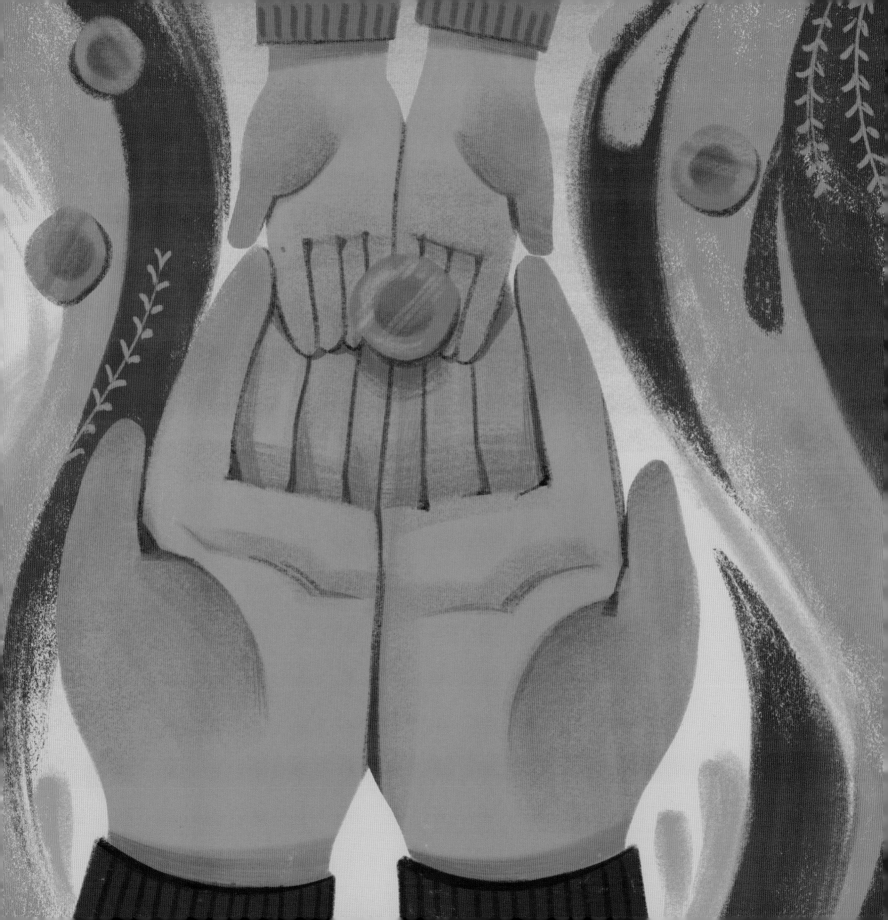

I told him about Armenia.

Author's Note

My sons are descendants of the Armenian orphan who inspired this book—his name is Michael. He survived the Armenian Genocide and went on to have several grandchildren, one of whom I married. For as long as I've known him, my husband has been trying to figure out his family's story, a puzzle with most of its pieces missing. He remembers a sadness in his grandfather's eyes and can only imagine what he might have gone through to arrive in Tripoli, Lebanon, all the way from his hometown of Everek, Armenia (now Develi, Turkey).

April 24, 1915, is the date widely recognized as the start of the Armenian Genocide. Most Armenians at that time were forced out of their homes and deported. They had to travel far, mostly on foot, through mountains and deserts, without food or water. It is estimated that 1.5 million Armenians lost their lives. Many children ended up in orphanages in neighboring countries. One of those children was my husband's grandfather. Like most survivors, he never found the words to tell his story.

Survivors often found the past too difficult to talk about. For many who went on to build new lives and start their own families, silence was also a way to keep their children safe from the trauma they had suffered. In the Armenian families I know, the Armenian Genocide is seldom openly discussed. There are whispers of it: a name of a town, of a distant relative in another country, of a friend's friend who might know something—pieces of an incomplete story. More questions than answers.

It saddens me that we can't shed more light on our children's great-grandfather's story, but my husband and I want our boys to know what happened to the Armenian people. We want them to tell their own children about the struggle, strength, and resilience of their ancestors so that their story may live on.

My children's great-grandfather Michael, whose story inspired this book, and his wife, Deebeh.

My sister-in-law Zarig and her great-aunt Satenig, one of the sisters portrayed in this story.

More than a hundred years later, we are in the midst of the biggest refugee crisis the world has ever known. The numbers can be overwhelming when we wonder how we might be able to help. I used to find myself asking, "What difference can I possibly make when the problem is so much bigger than I am?" But I like to think that even if you've helped just one person, to that person, you have made the whole difference.

To learn more about what you can do to help people in need in Armenia and around the world, visit the Near East Foundation: neareast.org.

Michael, his son Missak, and his grandson Haig (my husband).

Michael and his sisters started their journey in Everek, Armenia, and made their way to Tripoli, Lebanon. No one knows whether they took a boat when they reached the coast or if they walked to Aleppo, Syria, and then to Tripoli.

Michael, his daughter-in-law Ingrid, and Haig.

Illustrator's Note

All of my great-grandparents lived through the Armenian Genocide, and all found the resilience within themselves to create new lives while being separated from their families and homes.

We're still trying to piece together exactly what happened and how each part of our family ended up where they did. We have family photos with faces we're still trying to name, a family tree with giant gaps, and relatives we're discovering to this day. Many Armenians, like us, are trying to uncover their families' lost stories and reconnect across the diaspora.

I'm proud of what my family has overcome, and I'm even prouder that we've found ways to reunite with one another after all this time. I hope that by telling one story, we shed light not only on the events that so many Armenians went through but also on tragedies that others have faced, and still face, across generations.

My great-grandmother Vanuhi; my grandmother Hasmik; my mother, Archaluys (bottom middle); her sister, Adel (bottom left); and their cousin Vanouhi (bottom right).

My grandfather Byzant (left) and his brother, Garbis (right).

My grandfather Garabed.

A Brief History

At the beginning of World War I (1914–18), Western Armenia was part of the Ottoman Empire, a state formed by Turkish tribes in 1299. Before the war, and as the empire began to crumble, Armenians protested their unequal treatment and demanded regional autonomy.

In January 1915, after a lost battle against Russia, the empire accused Armenians of posing a pro-Russian national security threat. On April 24, 1915, a group of Armenian leaders and intellectuals— including politicians, doctors, bankers, lawyers, writers, and priests—were rounded up and later deported or executed. Many men and boys were separated from their families, and women, children, and the elderly were forced to leave their homes.

That was when the deportation marches began. Accompanied by gendarmes, or military police, hundreds of thousands of Armenians were forced to walk through the deserts of Syria without food or water. In that time, Greeks, Assyrians, and other Christian minorities were also being persecuted in the name of nationalism. Of the estimated 2 million Christians who lost their lives to the brutality of the Ottoman Empire between 1915 and 1923,* 1.5 million are believed to be Armenian.

Today, about 3 million Armenians reside in Armenia, which gained independence in 1991, and an additional estimated 8 million live around the world. The largest populations are in Russia, the United States, France, Georgia, Lebanon, and Iran.

*The end of the Armenian Genocide, like many genocides, is difficult to determine and often disputed. Although they were forced into the desert between 1915 and 1917, Armenians were still being targeted and driven out of their homes as Turkish nationalists were preparing to fight for the formation of the Turkish Republic, which was made official in 1923.

Some Facts about Armenia

- Armenia became the first Christian nation in 301 CE.
- Armenians celebrate Christmas on January 6.
- Yerevan, the capital of Armenia, is one of the world's oldest cities still inhabited today.
- Chess is taught in schools to children as young as six years old.
- Armenian family names often end in "-ian."
- The world's oldest leather shoe was found in a cave in Armenia; it is estimated to be 5,500 years old.
- A carpet woven by Armenian orphans in Ghazir, now in Lebanon, was offered to United States president Calvin Coolidge in 1925 as a symbol of gratitude for the United States' support during the genocide. It remains in the White House today.
- You might know some world-famous Armenians such as the Kardashians, Cher, Andre Agassi, Charles Aznavour, and Serj Tankian.

Glossary

Mante: Armenian dumplings

Baba: Armenian for "dad"

Hokis: Armenian for "my soul"

Nana: Term of endearment for "grandma"

Dada: Term of endearment for "grandpa"

Genocide: The killing of a group of people because of their race, religious beliefs, or culture. Raphael Lemkin coined the term in 1944, and the United Nations declared it a crime against humanity in 1948.

Selected Bibliography

Babkenian, Vicken. "Hollywood's First Celebrity Humanitarian That America Forgot." *The Armenian Weekly*, January 7, 2011. armenianweekly.com/2011/01/07/hollywoods-first-celebrity-humanitarian-that-america-forgot/.

Balakian, Peter. *Black Dog of Fate: A Memoir*. 1997. New edition, New York: Basic Books, 2009.

Blaylock, Josh, and Hoyt Silva. *Operation Nemesis: A Story of Genocide and Revenge*. Chicago: Devil's Due Entertainment, 2015.

Bryce, James. *The Treatment of Armenians in the Ottoman Empire, 1915–16*. New York and London: G. P. Putnam's Sons, 1916.

Miller, Donald E., and Lorna Touryan Miller. *Survivors: An Oral History of the Armenian Genocide*. Berkeley: University of California Press, 1993.

Morris, Benny, and Dror Ze'evi. *The Thirty-Year Genocide: Turkey's Destruction of Its Christian Minorities, 1894–1924*. Cambridge, MA: Harvard University Press, 2019.

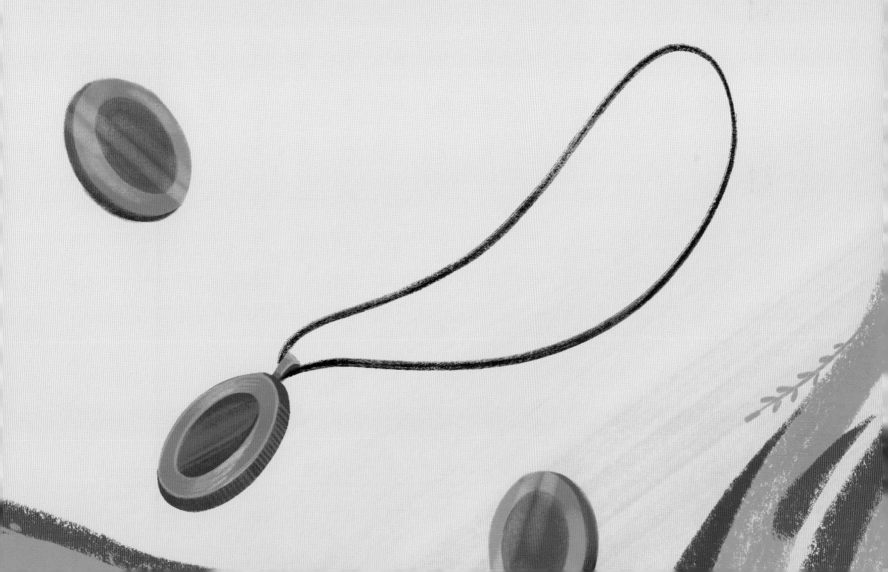